W9-CBR-412

HOW BEASTLY!

A Menagerie of Nonsense Poems

JANE YOLEN

Pictures by James Marshall

Wordsong
Boyds Mills Press

DEDICATED TO

Here are rhymes, a beastly crew,

Engaged in playing tricks for you.

I wrote them down with you in mind.

Do let me know which ones you find

In keeping with your "beastly" taste.
(I sign, your loving mom, in haste.)

Janet Yolen

Text copyright © 1980 by Jane Yolen
Illustrations copyright © 1980 by James Marshall

Published by Wordsong
Boyds Mills Press, Inc.
A Highlights Company
815 Church Street
Honesdale, Pennsylvania 18431
Printed in Mexico

Publisher Cataloging-in-Publication Data
Yolen, Jane.
        How beastly! : a menagerie of nonsense poems / by Jane Yolen ; pictures by
James Marshall.
[48]p. : ill. ; cm.
Originally published by William Collins Publishers, Inc., New York, 1980.
Summary: A collection of the author's nonsense poems about beastly creatures.
ISBN 1-56397-086-4
1. Animals, Mythical—Juvenile poetry. 2. Children's poetry, American. [1. Nonsense verses.
2. American poetry.] I. Marshall, James, 1942-1992, ill. II. Title.
811.54—dc20   1994
Library of Congress Catalog Card Number: 92-85036

The text of this book is set in 12-point Futura Book.
The illustrations are line drawings.
Distributed by St. Martin's Press

10 9 8 7 6 5 4 3 2

CONTENTS

THE SLUMMINGS

Once a year
The Slummings jump
Paw in paw
Into the dump.

.

THE FANGER

The Fanger's teeth are widely spaced
Inside his mouth, and strangely placed.
He cannot chew with any ease
The food that he prefers, like trees.
He must subsist instead on runny
Stuff like lemonade and honey.
Poor old Fanger, fed on goo
When he would *really* like to chew.
But oh, my dears, he must be cautious
Lest his dinner make him gnaw-tious.

THE SHIRK

The toothy Shirk swims lazily
Beneath the rainbow-colored sea.
It rarely has to move because
Its dinner swims into its jaws.

Upside down or rightside up
It does not have to work to sup.
And since it never has to work,
There is no one who likes the Shirk.

THE BLUFFALO

Oh, do not tease the Bluffalo
With quick-step or with shuffalo
When you are in a scuffalo
In Bluffalo's backyard.

For it has quite enoughalo
Of people playing toughalo
And when it gives a cuffalo
It gives it very hard.

But if by chance a scuffalo
Occurs twixt you and Bluffalo,
Pray tempt it with a truffalo
And catch it off its guard.

And while it eats that stuffalo
You can escape the Bluffalo
And with a huff and puffalo
Depart from its backyard.

THE OCTOPIE

Oh, see the Octopie inert
Upon the china plate.
It is a many-legged dessert
Which some folk underrate.
It seldom moves at dinner time
(For it has all it wants)
And so it is in great demand
At fancy restaurants.

THE CANTERPILLAR

The Canterpillar comes and goes
Upon her twice two hundred toes.
Her head is perched, with smile euphoric,
Upon a neck that's slim and Doric.
She gallops 'round at furious pace
But manages to lose each race,
For every single twinkling toe
Decides which way *it* wants to go.
Unless she gets her legs in sync,
I fear Ms. C. will be extinct.

THE SHLEPARD

A spotted beast the Shlepard is,
One of the feline race.
It leaps Nijinski-like in air
And lands—flat on its face.

A thing of beauty to behold,
Sheer poetry, not prose.
And when it leaps from tree to tree
It lands—flat on its nose.

THE SKANK

A tense ancestor of the skunk
Was the immortal Skank.
For bones and fragments of its skin
We've fossil hounds to thank.
They first discovered its remains
Deep in an ancient bank
And knew it for a skunk's grandpa
For oh my gosh, it stank.

THE WALRUST

Do not leave him out at night
Or near some dampish drains,
And never take him for a walk
On any day it rains
Because his baggy, wrinkled skin
Which looks like well-done crust
Is iron-hard and very thick
And is inclined to rust.

THE CENTERPEDE

The Centerpede on one flat foot
Stands on the dinner table.
It does not wink or blink or cough
As long as it is able.

It reaps a very sweet reward
For managing this feat,
For when the guests have left the room
It gets its turn to eat.

THE EDGEHOG

This creature dines on borderlines,
In bush, in shrub, in hedge.
It nests in tippy places, like
A jutting rock or ledge,
And never lives life to the full
But always on the edge.

THE PYTHONG

The Pythong ties itself in knots
But has a tiny brain
And so it cannot ever get
Itself untied again
Unless, at last, a very friendly
Hunter comes along
Who all unknowing soon undoes
The tiny-brained Pythong.
And that undoing soon undoes
The friendly hunter, for
Alas, the pea-brained Pythong
Is a deadly carnivore.

THE CROCODIAL

The dime goes in the Crocodial,
Crocodial, Crocodial,
It only takes a little while
Until your call goes through.

He chews the dime in little bits,
Little bits, little bits,
And then disgorges all the pits.
That's when your call goes through.

Don't be upset by his broad smile,
His broad smile, his broad smile,
He's a *dime*-atarian Crocodial,
Until your call goes through.

THE AARDWORT

Have you heard of the Aardwort,
A four-legged fungus
That quietly lives out
Its cycle among us?
It dines upon ants and
Occasional grasses
And never says no
To a germ as it passes.

THE PORCUPIN

Oh, do not needle Porcupin,
His rage is long, his patience thin,
A fight with him no one can win,
So don't get in the way.

His hair he wears both straight and long,
Each hair is like a sharpened prong,
So never do this beastie wrong
But let him have his say.

For when he gets into a fight
He doesn't throw a left or right,
He simply sews his foes up tight
And makes his getaway.

THE TAUGHTUS

The Taughtus is a Bahston beast
That climbs up Beacon Hill.
It started up before the Wah,*
In fact, it's climbing still.

It lectures calmly as it climbs
In accents soft and low,
But what it says and what it means
Nobody seems to know.

*Revolutionary, of course.

THE DINOSORE

Poor Dinosore, his body's big,
His tail it weighs a ton,
His head is full of bones and stones,
And when he tries to run

The pounding poundage gets him down.
He gasps and gasps some more.
His aching feet, they have him beat,
That's why he's Dinosore.

THE PIGUANA

Snout too little,
Tail too big,
Still it looks
A lot like pig.

Serve it hot
With wine or root,
Still it tastes
A lot like newt.

THE ALLIGATE

If you come to my house for a visit,
Be warned of a hideous fate,
For there in the alley before you
A terrible beast lies in wait.

Its head is just like a veranda.
Its mouth like a cavernous door,
And people who enter that gateway
Are never heard from anymore.

So if you come over to see me,
Remember that hideous fate,
And whatever you do, do not come by
The jaws of the fierce Alligate.

THE TIGIRTH

The Tigirth weighs an awful lot.
You think that it's a cat—it's not.

THE TUNER FISH

Far out at sea the mighty Tuner
Plays upon his scales.
He entertains the halibuts
But doesn't please the whales.

The whales prefer the deep, you see,
They like the hefty bass, *
The Tuner Fish sings tenor,
And that's high in any case.

*In fish circles, they pronounce the word
bass to rhyme with sass, and say the
poem this way:

The whales prefer the deep, you see,
They like the hefty bass,
The Tuner Fish's a tenor
And his school is upper class.

THE FAX

The Fax is gathered into groups
Like caucuses and boy scout troops.
The Fax is gathered into throngs
At football games and sing-alongs.
The Fax is gathered into clumps
In salad bowls and garbage dumps.
The Fax is gathered into crowds
Of daffodils and thunder clouds.
The Fax is gathered into groups
And droops.

JANE YOLEN is the distinguished author of more than one hundred books for children, young adults, and adults. Her *Owl Moon*, illustrated by John Schoenherr, won the 1988 Caldecott Medal. She is the author of *All in the Woodland Early*, *An Invitation to the Butterfly Ball*, *Jane Yolen's Mother Goose Songbook*, and *Street Rhymes Around the World*, all available from Boyds Mills Press. Ms. Yolen lives in Hatfield, Massachusetts.

JAMES MARSHALL was the illustrator of more than seventy books for children. He was best known for his series about hippopotamuses George and Martha; mischievous Fox; Miss Nelson; and the Stupid family. He also illustrated retellings of classic fairy tales, including the Caldecott Honor Book *Goldilocks*.